CHRISTOPHER PIKE

SPOOKSVILLE ™ #16

TIME TERROR

A MINSTREL® BOOK

Published by POCKET BOOKS
New York   London   Toronto   Sydney   Tokyo   Singapore

A MINSTREL PAPERBACK *Original*

A Minstrel Book published by
POCKET BOOKS, a division of Simon & Schuster Inc.
1230 Avenue of the Americas, New York, NY 10020

ISBN: 0-671-00264-3

First Minstrel Books printing May 1997

10 9 8 7 6 5 4 3 2 1

Cover art by John Youssi

Printed in the U.S.A.

SPOOKSVILLE #16

TIME TERROR

The gang was outside the movie theater, and they had just voted to see if they should go in to the movie or do something else that Friday evening. Sally Wilcox and Bryce Poole voted for the movie; Watch was undecided; Cindy Makey and Adam Freeman voted against. The movie was called *Invasion of the Horrible Thing*—Spooksville's theater played only horror movies, of course—and Sally and Bryce had heard it was really good. Adam and Cindy were tired of horror movies. They had seen nothing else since moving to Spooksville that summer. Why, even at the video store it was only possible to rent horror movies.

"But what are we going to do if we don't go to the movies?" Sally complained. Sally liked to complain; she considered it a virtue, like having an assertive personality. Sally was tall and skinny. She had long brown hair that she wore with bangs that always fell in her eyes.

"We could play Monopoly," Cindy suggested. Cindy, except when she was fighting with Sally, was the most soft-spoken one in the group. She had blond hair and blue eyes and had a horrible crush on Adam, which he tried to forget.

"Monopoly is different in this town than in others," Sally warned. "If you get a bad roll of the dice you don't go directly to jail without passing Go or collecting two hundred dollars, you lose one of your fingers. Spooksville's game comes with a tiny guillotine."

"I never heard anything more ridiculous in my life," Cindy said. "Who'd play such a game?"

"It's a big seller around Halloween," Watch said. Watch was known for always wearing four watches and having no last name. Watch added, "That might explain why so many people have trouble getting dressed up to go out that night. They don't have any fingers left."

"We could play chess," Adam suggested. He was relatively new to town but was already the leader of the group, largely because he was so brave and kind. Of course, he never thought of himself that way. Sally snickered at his suggestion.

"We can't play chess with Watch," she said. "No one can beat Watch. Even a computer can't beat him. It's no fun."

"Even I can't beat him," Bryce said seriously. "And I am the unofficial world junior chess champion." Bryce was tall and dark haired. He'd lived in Spooksville all his life but had only recently become friends with the gang. They liked him, except when he was bragging, which he was prone to do.

"But I think seeing nothing but horror films is ruining our minds," Cindy complained. "I know they give me nightmares."

"How can a silly horror film disturb you when the whole world is filled with horror?" Sally demanded. "Look at the starving children in Africa. Look at the evil dictators in the Middle East. I think a good horror film is a relief from the unending suffering in the world."

Cindy was thoughtful. "When you put it that way, I see your point."

"What's this movie about anyway?" Adam wanted to know.

Bryce spoke with enthusiasm. "It's about some aliens who come to earth and implant mind-altering devices in people in a small town. These controlled people then go around murdering innocent young kids with laserlike swords."

"Hey," Sally said. "That already happened in this town. Are you sure this isn't a documentary?"

"It sounds like a reasonable story," Watch said. "But I'll do whatever you guys want to do."

"You're so democratic," Sally said sarcastically. "You should be more opinionated. You need a stronger sense of will."

Watch shrugged and pushed his thick glasses up on his nose. "I enjoy any movie now that I can see it." Only recently did the local town witch, Ms. Ann Templeton, improve both Watch's eyesight and his glasses. Watch had been more than half-blind most of his life, but now he could see almost as well as the rest of them.

Adam sighed. "I suppose we can see the movie. But someone's going to have to buy my ticket. I already spent my allowance."

"I'll buy your ticket, Adam," Cindy said sweetly.

Sally jeered. "Hey, guys, it'll be like they're going on a date. Maybe we shouldn't sit with them. Maybe they want to be alone. Maybe—"

"Quiet," Adam interrupted. "We're too young to date."

Cindy looked disappointed. "How old do we have to be?"

As a group they walked up to the theater box office. The young woman who sold the tickets was real scary looking. Her hair was long and black and she had the darkest lips and the palest eyes. Sally said she was a part-time vampire, whatever that meant. All the others knew was that her nails were long and sharp and looked as if they'd been dipped in blood. She smiled as they approached her. Her eyes were as green as a cat's.

"Our local stars," she said in a silky voice. "What can I do for you?"

Watch handed over their money. "We would like five tickets to this evening's show."

The weird woman took their money but then paused. "How old are you guys?" she asked.

"Twelve," Watch said. "Why?"

"You know this film is rated *F*," she said. "I need to know if you are old enough to see it before I sell you tickets."

"I never heard of an *F*-rated film," Cindy said. "What does the *F* stand for?"

The vampirish woman leaned closer. "The *F* stands for *Fatal*. Which means this film can scare you to death if you're not old enough to withstand the horror and the gore."

Sally chuckled. "Listen, lady, we may only be twelve but we've lived through enough horror to wipe out a dozen vampires like you."

The woman seemed pleased to be called a vampire.

"So, you have heard about me?" she asked.

"Of course," Sally said. "I know you try to drip some of your blood on the popcorn, instead of putting butter on it. You're trying to make more vampires. You're trying to take over this town. But it's not going to happen. We just want you to know that ahead of time. And we just want butter and salt on our popcorn."

The strange woman did not seem to be offended. "You realize that at this theater the popcorn is free but the butter and salt are five bucks."

Watch pulled out another wad of bills. "We have it. Just make sure our popcorn has no red fluid on it."

The vampirish woman laughed and fingered her long black hair. "You kids will join me eventually. The whole town will. It's the latest fad."

Sally grabbed their tickets. "Compared to the monsters we've had to deal with, you vampires are nothing. We'll take care of you when we get around to it."

The woman laughed again.

They went inside and watched the movie.

It was awfully scary.

They loved it, including Cindy and Adam.

2

After the film, they exited through the rear doorway into the alleyway. There was a commotion going on in the lobby, and they didn't want to get involved. It sounded as if the vampire woman was trying to drink the blood of a young couple. Sometimes in Spooksville it was better to stay out of other people's business. Even Adam, who loved to save everyone from harm, was finally learning that.

It was in the alley that they first saw the Time Toy.

It was off to their right, hidden in the shadows.

They didn't call it that at first, of course. As they stepped over to it they thought that it was just a cool-looking robot. It was designed like a scary warrior, obviously made of metal, painted orange, and maybe two feet tall. For some reason it had a large yellow clock in its belly, which didn't go with the rest of the design. There was a faint white glow by its mouth and eyes, as if it were battery powered and turned on. They gathered around it and studied it for a moment before speaking.

"Cool," Watch said finally.

"I wonder who left it here," Cindy said.

"Finders keepers," Sally said as she touched the top of it.

"We're not going to take it," Adam said. "Remember what happened when we tried taking the Wishing Stone home. We ended up on a slave planet surrounded by hostile aliens."

"That was different," Sally said. "That was an alien device planted to trap unsuspecting humans. This is just a great-looking toy."

"But it doesn't belong to us," Cindy said.

"If the people who owned it wanted it they

wouldn't have left it here," Sally said. "It's obvious someone dumped it here to get rid of it." She ran her fingers over the rim of the toy's orange metal hat. "I'm going to take it home."

"That's stealing," Cindy hissed.

"You're such a moralist," Sally said as she crouched beside it with Watch. He put a hand on the clock in the toy's belly and began to move the hands. Inside the toy made a faint humming sound.

"It's definitely turned on," Watch said. "But I wonder what it does."

"It probably just walks and talks," Sally said.

"I don't think so," Watch said as he continued to fiddle with the clock. "I think this timepiece is central to the toy's function." He pointed to a series of three dials on top of the toy's head. They were each numbered one through ten. The humming sound continued, growing in volume. The intensity of the white light in the eyes and mouth also increased. Watch added, "I think these dials are connected to the clock."

Curious, Adam knelt down by the toy. "Maybe the hands on the clock just wind the toy."

Watch disagreed. "It was running when we found it. For that reason I don't think it has to be wound. No, I think it's battery powered." He studied the back and sides, searching for a battery panel. Then he touched the bolts that protruded from the thing's neck. The humming accelerated. "I just don't know where you put in the batteries."

Sally stood and tried to lift it. She groaned. "It's heavy."

"Good. You won't be able to carry it home," Cindy said.

"Would you get off your high horse," Sally said, insulted. "I'm not stealing it. I'm just taking it home to take care of it."

Bryce was also crouching beside it now. "It seems to be warming up. I think touching the hands on the clock triggered it. It keeps humming louder, and that light in its mouth and eyes is really getting bright."

Watch nodded and stood up. "I think we should leave it here."

Sally was indignant. "Why? It's a totally great toy."

"I've changed my opinion. This can't be powered by ordinary batteries," Watch explained, putting his hand out to help pull Sally up. The rest of them stood and backed up slightly. Sally, as usual, was proving stubborn. Watch continued, "It definitely has too much power to be running off batteries. And until we know what its source of power is, we shouldn't fool with it."

Sally stood reluctantly. The glow from the toy now bathed the entire alleyway in light and the hum must have been audible from the street. Even Sally appeared slightly concerned.

"It doesn't seem like a toy you'd buy in a store," she admitted.

Watch motioned for them to back up farther. "I've never seen anything like this. I even wonder if it's from this planet."

Sally snickered. "Now you're being ridiculous. Not every cool thing we find has to be from another world. Why, I bet this thing—"

Sally never finished her sentence.

The humming suddenly increased a hundred-fold.

There was a flash of bright light.

Then they were all flying, or falling, or both.

They saw exploding stars, spinning planets.

It seemed as if they were caught in the center of a galactic hurricane.

It was terrifying. More scary than any horror film.

And it seemed to go on forever.

3

But forever is a long time, even in a place as strange as Spooksville. Eventually the weird visual and sound distortions stopped, and they found themselves standing at the base of a green hill that overlooked the sea. There were a few buildings in a primitive settlement around them. All the buildings were built of rough-sawn lumber and stone. Smoke poured from the chimney of the nearest one. Out on the water they saw a sailboat. The light was dim; it was near sunset. The sun, in fact, was the only thing that seemed familiar.

Yet that wasn't exactly true. The hills behind

the settlement were familiar. They were the same hills that always stood around Spooksville, as were the trees. The only trouble was, their town was gone.

"Where are we?" Sally asked in wonder. "What happened?"

"I told you to leave that toy alone," Cindy complained, frightened.

"We're OK," Adam said quickly, trying to calm them all down. "Whatever has happened hasn't harmed us."

"Wrong. My wits have been harmed," Cindy said.

Bryce gazed around with a grin on his face. He alone seemed to be enjoying himself. "The toy transported us somewhere," he muttered.

They only realized right then that the toy was still standing in front of them. But it had stopped humming and glowing. It stood perfectly still like an ordinary toy on a department store shelf. Watch knelt beside it but didn't touch it.

"We haven't been transported anywhere," he said quietly.

"What?" Sally said. "You're wrong. We're not in Spooksville anymore."

Watch glanced up at them. "But we are in Spooksville. Look around, all the major physical features of the area are the same. All that has changed are the buildings and the number of people."

"I'd call those substantial changes," Sally said.

Watch stood and gestured to the few buildings, and to the boat out at sea. "This is Spooksville, but it's Spooksville a couple of hundred years ago. This toy is a Time Toy. It's transported us not through space but through time."

His remark stunned them, and yet, no one could argue with the facts. The more they got their bearings, the more obvious the truth became. Bryce nodded his head in approval.

"You're right, Watch. As always," he added. "We haven't changed our position at all. We're still the same distance from the ocean, about a quarter of a mile. But do you really think we're back that far in time?"

Watch nodded. "At least. These are obviously eighteenth-century structures. I know boats as well. That one out on the water looks as if it were constructed in the mid-eighteenth century." Watch next pointed to the toy. "The position of the dials on top of the toy's head—in relation to the position of the arms on the clock—probably determine how far back in time we're transported."

"Cool," Sally said, excited. "Let's explore. I've always wondered what it would be like to live back in this time."

Watch shook his head. "We must not do anything like that. We can't risk upsetting the time line."

"What's that?" Cindy asked.

"It's a theory about the way time works," Bryce explained. "It's based on the idea of causality. For example, if you go back in time and murder your grandmother when she was young, you set up a paradox. If she is dead you can't have been born. Therefore you can't have murdered her. Yet you did, which is impossible. You see the difficulties if you tamper with the past?"

Cindy frowned. "I guess."

"But I don't want to murder anyone," Sally said. "I just want to talk to a few people and tell them what the future's like. I mean, gimme a break. Why would I want to hurt my dear sweet grandmother?"

"Bryce was just using that as an example of what can happen if we tamper with the past," Watch said. "Simply talking to someone back in this time about the future might be enough to change the future. Indeed, someone just has to look at us and things might change."

"We're not that good-looking," Sally muttered.

"This makes sense to me," Adam said. "We have to move carefully. We're treating this thing like a toy when it's obviously much more than that. I say we figure out a way to reprogram it and have it teleport us back to our own time."

Watch again crouched beside the Time Toy. "That's easier said than done," he muttered. "I accidentally set the time coordinates to this time. But I'm not sure how to set them back to our time. The way these dials are set up in relationship to the clock—I don't think they follow a calendar."

Bryce knelt beside him. "But the clock is a standard clock, which makes me think the device was designed to be used solely on this planet. That should give us a starting point from which to recalibrate the dials."

"Just don't send us farther back in time," Cindy said. "I don't want to run into any dinosaurs. I had enough trouble when that pterodactyl appeared last summer and swept me away to its prehistoric nest."

Sally waved her hand. "That was just a big lizard bird. I wasn't afraid of it."

Cindy was insulted. "You started screaming your head off the second you saw it. If I hadn't protected you, it would have got you. And I doubt that you would have survived."

"When have you ever protected me from anything?" Sally asked. "I have to hold your hand and wipe your tears anytime we get going on a real good adventure."

"Would you two stop?" Adam said, studying the toy with Watch and Bryce. "We're in a serious situation here, and we all have to work together."

Sally waved her hand again. "Watch will figure out how to reset the device. He's great at that kind of stuff."

"I'm grateful for the vote of confidence," Watch

said as he cautiously touched the top dials. "But it's possible I might transport us to a time before earth existed."

"What would happen to us then?" Cindy asked.

"We'd die," Bryce said grimly. "In the cold vacuum of space."

"Cheery," Cindy muttered.

While Watch and Bryce examined the Time Toy, Sally decided to go for a walk. But Adam wouldn't let her go far.

"You heard what Watch and Bryce said about paradoxes," he told her.

Sally was impatient. "We can at least hike up to the top of that hill and look around. That couldn't possibly hurt anything. All the people seem to be indoors."

"Do so at your own risk," Watch muttered.

"And the risk of the rest of the world," Bryce added.

Adam was undecided. He didn't see what harm it could do just to look. He was also curious about the rest of the settlement.

"All right," he agreed finally. "But if we see anyone we run back here. We don't talk."

"Agreed," Sally said.

Together Adam, Cindy, and Sally hiked up to the top of the nearest hill. The grass was high and thick, and they had to struggle to make it. But once they were at the summit, they had an unobstructed view of the two-hundred-year-old Spooksville. To their immense surprise they saw that the church they knew and the town cemetery were already in place. The witch's castle was also present. Although smaller than it was back in their time, there was no mistaking it. The castle even had the same moat.

"Wow," Sally said. "I think we're back in the time of Madeline Templeton."

"Who was she?" Cindy asked. "I forget."

"She is called the original founder of our town," Sally explained. "She was Ann Templeton's great-great-great-great-grandmother. She was supposed to be the most powerful witch of them all." Sally nodded. "The people in this town eventually put her to death."

"They can't be very friendly," Cindy muttered.

"They're probably more superstitious than anything," Adam said.

"Then they picked a great place to settle down," Sally remarked. "I wonder if this town is as spooky as ours. I bet it is."

"Maybe the spookiness started back in this time," Adam said.

Sally wore a fiendish expression. "What I wouldn't give to know."

Adam put his hand on her shoulder. "We've had our look. Now we're going back to the others. We're not here to have an adventure. This is supposed to be Friday night. We were just going to see a movie and take it easy."

Sally nodded reluctantly and walked down the hill with Adam and Cindy.

"But you never know when you will stumble upon an adventure in this town," she muttered.

Watch and Bryce had figured out—they hoped—how to reset the dials to transport them back to their own time. The toy was turned on and making noise.

"But we just made an educated guess," Watch warned. "What we do next could kill us. We really could end up in the mouth of a dinosaur."

"But they don't have TV in this time," Cindy

tried to joke, although it was obvious she was nervous. "I'll miss all my favorites series. We have to risk it."

Watch gestured for them to stand in front of the Time Toy.

"I believe we have to be zapped by the thing's light to be transported," he said. "As you can see and hear, we already have it humming and glowing again. But I think it was when I accidentally touched the neck bolts that it really moved us in time. I'll do the same thing again." Watch leaned over and pressed on the bolts. The humming and the intensity of the light immediately increased. Watch stepped back and added, "Hold on to your hats."

Cindy cringed beside Adam. "Maybe we should hold on to each other. I'd hate to get lost in time."

They were all more scared than they were willing to admit. At Cindy's suggestion they linked hands. Sally even grasped Cindy's hand and Cindy squeezed Sally's fingers tight. The humming began to drown out every other sound. The light pouring out of the toy's eyes and mouth was blinding.

Then there was a huge burst of light and sound.
Once more they fell, they flew.

It was as if they spun above the entire universe.

The galaxies twirled. Time seemed to lose all
meaning.

They could still see one another but each person
seemed light-years away.

Then there was another blinding and deafening
burst.

They were standing in the alleyway behind the
theater.

Inside the building it sounded as if the weird
vampire woman was still trying to talk the young
couple into sharing their blood with her. Well,
perhaps *talk* was too gentle a word. It sounded as if
she were insisting on receiving a transfusion before the night was through. In either case, they
were back in their time at what they believed was
almost the exact moment they had left.

"It's good we didn't come back a few minutes
early," Sally said. "We might have run into ourselves."

Watch spoke seriously. "That would have been
a disaster of major proportions."

"What do you mean?" Adam asked.

Watch shrugged. "For all we know meeting ourselves—actually touching ourselves—might cause the world to explode. I don't know enough about time travel to say for sure. I just know it's an experiment I wouldn't want to try."

"But you knew enough to get us home again," Cindy said, giving Watch a big hug. "What would we do without you?"

Sally patted him on the back. "You're the best, Watch."

Watch glowed with obvious pleasure although he seemed embarrassed as well. "Bryce contributed to figuring it out," he said. "He deserves half the credit."

Sally laughed and winked at Bryce. "We'll give it to him later."

"I don't need praise," Bryce said quietly. "I just do what needs to be done. That you're all safe and well is thanks enough for me."

They all laughed together at Bryce.

"Oh brother," Sally groaned. "Please don't be such a martyr. We all need some praise now and then. We're all human—you, too, although you hate to admit it." She patted Bryce on the back and even rubbed his head. "We formally thank you as well, Bryce, for saving our miserable lives. Really, you guys did a great job working together." She nodded to the toy. "Now I want you all to help me carry this thing home."

They stared at her in amazement.

"After what we just went through you want to take it home?" Cindy asked.

"Of course," Sally said. "I mean, we can't just leave it here. What if someone finds it who doesn't know about the dangers of paradoxes and causality? They might transport themselves back in time to the cavemen and destroy all of modern civilization."

"Sally does have a point. We really can't let anyone else use it," Watch admitted.

"But are you going to use it?" Adam asked Sally. "You're reckless. I think you're the last person in the group who should be put in charge of it."

Sally was insulted. "I swear I won't use it. And I resent you calling me reckless. I am merely impulsive. There is a profound difference."

"I wouldn't mind taking care of it," Bryce said.

"Oh yeah," Sally said sarcastically. "You'd probably use it to go back in time to try to improve your bloodline."

"I doubt my bloodline could be improved," Bryce said with a straight face. "All my ancestors were brilliant in their own way."

"Look," Sally said. "I just want to stow it in my garage. My family has the biggest one. It's jammed with stuff so no one will ever find it in there. And I promise not to use it to fool with time."

"Why don't we just bury it somewhere?" Cindy suggested.

Watch shook his head. "That's not a good idea. Someone, perhaps even in a future generation, might find it. No, I think we have to take personal responsibility for it."

"Then it's settled," Sally said. "It is going in my garage."

It was settled. Sally could be insistent when she wanted something badly enough. Together they helped carry it to Sally's garage, where they stowed it in the corner beneath an old wool rug.

Then they each said good night and started toward home. Sally went inside and watched TV with her parents.

But later, when Sally's parents were sound asleep, she sneaked back out to the garage. She took the old rug off the Time Toy. Then she ever so carefully touched the arms on the clock.

A bright light went off.

4

It was Adam; he had turned on the garage light. Sally stared at him, shocked. She had her hand on her heart.

"You almost scared me to death," she gasped. "What are you doing here?"

Adam nodded grimly and stepped toward her.

"To see if you were going to honor your promise," he said. "But I can see we cannot trust you with this thing. Really, Sally, I'm disappointed in you."

Sally stood. "Why? I only promised not to fool

with time. I didn't say I wouldn't try to go back in time again."

Adam spoke firmly. "They're one and the same. You can't travel into the past without upsetting the present. Watch and Bryce explained all that. You should know better."

"They were being overly dramatic," Sally said. "True, if we went into the past and accidentally killed someone or something, that would be awful. It would change a whole family line. But if we just went back and observed things from a distance it couldn't do any harm."

Adam was curious in spite of himself. "What is it you want to observe?"

Sally's eyes were wide. "The time we were just in. The beginning of Spooksville. All my life I've been trying to solve the mystery of this town. Why is it so spooky? What is so special about it? Well, I think the answer must lie in Spooksville's beginning." She gripped his arm. "Think about it, Adam. I know you're an explorer by nature. We can beam ourselves back there and see just what it was that Madeline Templeton did to this place."

"But how do we know she did anything to

Spooksville?" Adam said. "You have a habit of blaming our present-day Ann Templeton for everything that goes wrong in town. It's possible her great-great-great-great-grandmother had nothing to do with how this place turned out."

"That's impossible. It's Madeline Templeton's tombstone that opens the Secret Path. It was she who cursed the Derby Tree so that its leaves are always bloodred. Her influence is everywhere in this town. I think it was she who cast the original curse on this city." Sally was thoughtful. "It's possible that if we go back in time and stop her, this town will be much safer to live in."

"Now you're talking about what Watch said we couldn't do," Adam warned. "Under no circumstances can we do anything to alter the past."

Sally waved her hand. "All right, all right. But let's go back and observe. We have to do it, Adam, it's a once in a lifetime chance." She took his hand. "Please say you'll come with me? We don't have to tell the others. They don't have to know."

Adam was uncomfortable. "But we always do things as a group."

Sally spoke quietly but seriously. "The fewer of

us who go back in time, the less chance there'll be that time will be altered. I mean, I think it would be a mistake to take Cindy with us. She'd probably get a crush on some guy back there and want to stay."

"I hardly think that would happen."

"But my point's a good one. Two is a good number. Let's do it. Let's do it now."

Adam let go of her and knelt beside the Time Toy.

"I'm not even sure I know how to work this thing," he said.

Sally crouched beside him. "I know how to use it to get us there and back. I studied what Watch did closely, how he set the dials. I've already set it to take us back to the place we were before."

"No," Adam corrected her. "We may end up in the same time but we won't end up in the same place. We are now in your garage, not in the alleyway behind the theater. When we go back in time, we'll be in the spot where your house now stands. We have to keep that in mind."

"Why?" Sally asked.

"Because where this house is, back then, might

be located where there are more people. There might be a greater chance we'll be seen."

"You are exaggerating the danger," Sally said. "If we appear in a bad situation we can immediately reprogram the Time Toy and come back to the here and now."

Adam considered. "It should be OK."

Sally was excited. "You'll come with me?"

"Will you go without me if I don't come?"

"Of course. I am a self-sufficient person."

Adam sighed. "All right, I'll go. But at the first sign of any danger we return here. And we keep our contact with people to a minimum. Agreed?"

"Agreed." Sally touched the bolts coming out of the toy's neck. Right away it began to hum and glow. They both stood in front of it, holding hands.

"I just hope we don't materialize inside a rock," Adam muttered.

Sally paled. "I wish you hadn't said that."

It was too late to make any difference.

The Time Toy hummed, the bright light flashed.

Then they were flying through the cosmos.

Stars formed and died around them.

A million worlds rushed by.

The sensation was terrifying and wonderful.

When it stopped they were standing in the middle of a dirt road, the Time Toy in front of them. It appeared undisturbed. Unfortunately they couldn't say the same thing for their states of mind. The road on which they had appeared wasn't deserted. They were, in fact, surrounded by men and women in eighteenth-century attire who were staring at them in horror. It was slightly later than the last time they had come—near dark now. The people carried lanterns that lit up the road, which seemed to run through the very heart of town. An old man with a cruel face, a thin mustache, and a black patch over one eye spoke in a thick accent that sounded like a mixture of English and Spanish. But they could understand him well enough.

His meaning was painfully clear.

"Witches!" he cried with his lantern held high. "More witches! Grab them, men! Throw them in the prison! We will burn them with that cursed Madeline Templeton tomorrow morning!"

The people rushed them.

There was no time to reset the Time Toy.

Sally screamed but Adam just bowed his head. It was ironic, he thought. Because a moment ago in Sally's twentieth-century garage they had thought they had all the time in the world. What fools they were.

Now they were prisoners of the past.

Soon to be burned as witches.

5

Cindy was getting ready for bed when she got a call from Adam's father. Mr. Freeman was wondering if Cindy knew where his son was.

"He hasn't come home?" Cindy asked.

"No," Mr. Freeman said. He was a nice man even if he was kind of nerdy. "We haven't seen him. Weren't you kids going to a movie?"

"We saw the early show. The last time I saw Adam he was walking away from Sally's house. I thought he was going straight home."

"He's probably with Watch then. I'll call his house."

Cindy felt a stab of anxiety. "No, wait, Mr. Freeman. Let me get hold of Watch. I can find Adam faster than you."

The man chuckled softly. "I'm sure you're right. You kids are amazing, the way you stick together. Friends are what matter most in this world."

"I feel very fortunate to have such close friends," Cindy said.

"How do you like living in Springville?"

Mr. Freeman, of course, called Spooksville by its official name. The man had no idea of the adventures his son and friends had every other week. If he had he would have got his family out of town that very night. Cindy had to strain to maintain a normal voice as she answered.

"It's an interesting place," she said. "It's never boring."

"That's what Adam says. But he never tells me what you guys do all the time."

"Oh. We get around." Like to other planets and other times, Cindy thought.

"That's great. I still remember what it was

like to be a kid. Let me know when you find Adam."

"I will, Mr. Freeman. I'll call you soon."

They exchanged goodbyes. Cindy called Watch immediately and explained that Adam was missing.

"He probably went back to Sally's house," Watch remarked.

"Why do you say that?" she asked.

"I was thinking of doing the same thing myself."

"Because you don't trust Sally with the Time Toy?"

"Exactly," Watch said.

"I want to call her," Cindy said.

"No. Her parents are probably in bed already. Let's not disturb them. Let's walk over there and see what Adam and Sally are up to. We'll take Bryce with us. I doubt if he has gone to bed yet. We can swing by his house on the way over and pick him up."

"But you think they're OK, don't you?" Cindy asked, worried.

"I would prefer to see them with my own eyes than to have to think about it."

Bryce was not in bed—night owl that he was. He was only too happy to join them on their late-night exploratory hike. But he didn't seem overly worried about Adam and Sally.

"If Adam did go back to Sally's house," he said, "he'd never have let her try more time travel."

"Sally can be pretty convincing," Cindy warned.

"That's true," Watch said. "We should never have let her take the Time Toy in the first place."

When they reached Sally's house they first peered in her bedroom window. It was dark in the room but obviously she wasn't there. Next they quietly entered the side door of the garage. Cindy was relieved to see the Time Toy there, standing in the middle of the floor.

"At least we know they didn't take it into the past," she said.

Watch, on the other hand, wasn't so sure. He stepped up to the device.

"Why is the Time Toy sitting out?" he asked. "We put it under that rug there."

"Sally must have come out here to see it again," Bryce suggested.

"But where are Sally and Adam?" Watch asked. "They wouldn't go out together, not this late."

"What are you trying to say?" Cindy asked.

"That they might have used the Time Toy, after all," Watch said.

"But it's right here in front of us," Bryce said.

Watch held up a finger. "We know *a* Time Toy is right here in front of us. But it's possible that the device exists in many times. For example, when we went into the past after the movie this evening, how do we know the device did not continue to exist in the alleyway even while we had it with us in the past?"

"That's an interesting theory," Bryce said. "But it's only that. I still think Adam and Sally must be around here somewhere."

Cindy was shaking her head. "No, I think

Watch is right. Sally might be foolish sometimes but she wouldn't have left this thing out where her parents could find it. Sally is very secretive when it comes to her parents."

"But she'd have to be the biggest fool of all to go back into the past," Bryce pointed out.

"If she had had Adam with her she might have felt safe," Watch said.

"But Adam would never have gone," Bryce insisted.

"I'm not so sure about that," Watch said. "I told Adam not to go for a walk when we were back in time and he did. Now that was an innocent thing to do, and obviously no harm came of it. But he hiked up the hill with Sally and Cindy because he was curious to see what the rest of the town looked like. Adam is an extremely curious person. If Sally pushed the right button in him, he might have let her talk him into taking another trip into the past."

Bryce remained unconvinced. "The Time Toy is still here. That must mean—"

Bryce didn't have a chance to finish his sentence.

He just vanished. In the blink of an eye.

Yet there was no bright flash of light.

Cindy and Watch both jumped.

"Oh no!" Cindy gasped, backing away from the toy. "It must have turned itself on!"

Watch stared at the toy. "But there's no humming sound. There's no light."

"But Bryce is gone," Cindy cried. "He must be in the past."

Watch shook his head. "It might be worse than that for him. He might be . . . He might be . . ." Watch stuttered and then frowned. "What was I about to say?" he asked.

"You said he might be," Cindy began. "Wait a second, who were you talking about?"

"I don't know. I'm asking you."

"You must have been talking about Adam," Cindy said, feeling confused. There was something wrong with their situation, but she couldn't pinpoint what it was. "He must have gone back in time with Sally."

Watch was also confused. "But I'm sure we weren't talking about Adam, but about some other guy."

"What other guy? Who else do we know?"

"I don't know," Watch said. "But it seemed someone else was here a moment ago."

"No," Cindy protested. "We came over here together, just the two of us."

Watch continued to think. "But we're talking about time travel here. If Adam and Sally have gone into the past, maybe they've already done something that made one of us cease to exist."

"But we're here. We exist. Nothing has changed."

"That's my point. We don't know if anything has changed. How could we know? For all we know we came over here with three other friends and they've all been wiped out by what Sally and Adam did in the past."

"But we have no other close friends besides Sally and Adam," Cindy said.

"We don't *now*. But if the past has been changed, then our memories—as they are now—would also have been changed." Watch paused. "I'm sure I was talking about someone other than Adam. I had his name on the tip of my tongue."

"Who?"

"The person who has been wiped out by Adam and Sally. Look, we have no choice. We have to go into the past to try to correct what they've done to our time."

"But we don't know what they did," Cindy said.

"Yes. But they might know. We have to find them." Watch knelt beside the Time Toy. "It looks to me as if Sally reset the dials and clock to match the time we traveled to earlier. All we have to do is turn it on and we should be back with them."

"Why don't we set the clock a few minutes before then?" Cindy said. "That way we can arrive on the scene and rescue them before they mess things up."

"Good idea." Watch altered the clock face slightly. Then he stood up and held out his hand. "Are you ready? I am going to turn it on."

Cindy stared at him strangely. "Watch?"

"What?"

"Don't you wear glasses?"

"No. I've never worn glasses. Why do you ask?"

She kept staring at him. "I could swear you used to wear glasses."

"I have twenty-twenty vision. I can see anything." He paused as he looked at her. "Oh no," he muttered.

"What's wrong?" Cindy asked.

"You have long red hair."

Cindy touched her hair. "I have always had long red hair."

"Are you sure?"

"Of course. It's my pride and joy." She stopped. "You're not saying they have done something in the past that has changed the way I look? That's impossible."

"But you're saying I used to wear glasses."

"No. I was wrong." Cindy strained to remember. "I don't know where I got that idea. You've never worn glasses. And my hair has always been red. Nothing has changed. We're OK."

Watch was worried. "We can't be certain of anything. We have to get back into the past. We have to get Sally and Adam back into the present." Watch added, "If they even recognize us anymore."

Watch set the Time Toy on.

It hummed and glowed.

They held each other close.

There was another flash of light and sound.

They vanished from Sally's garage.

The Time Toy remained where it was.

6

Sally and Adam were in a desperate situation. Not only were they chained to a stone wall in a stinking dungeon, they had Madeline Templeton sitting cross-legged across from them in a neighboring cell. She was dressed entirely in black and had her eyes closed as if she were in a trance or something. Incredibly, she looked just like Ann Templeton, the same age even. Only she had long red hair instead of dark hair. But since she hadn't spoken to them, or even looked at them, they thought she was probably an undesirable character.

"I can't believe we're going to be burned to death with her," Sally said. "Can't they see we're nothing like her?"

"We did appear out of nowhere," Adam remarked. "That would make us suspicious in their eyes. Plus we had that weird-looking Time Toy with us."

"I wonder what they did with it."

"Who knows? I wouldn't be surprised if they were afraid to touch it."

Sally tugged uselessly at her chains. "They weren't afraid to touch us. Do you know that old man pulled out a ton of my hair when he grabbed us?"

"That must have hurt."

Sally sighed. "It still hurts. But I don't suppose I'm allowed to complain. It's my fault we're in this situation."

"I've been trying hard not to mention that," Adam said.

"I'm sorry. Me and my big mouth, huh?"

"It's got us into difficult situations before," Adam agreed.

"Well, there's no way we can let them burn us at the stake. What are we going to do?"

"Maybe we should appeal to Madeline Templeton for help," Adam suggested. "Her powers are legendary."

"There are guards right outside. They might hear us talking to her. I'd rather they didn't think we were in with her."

"Do we have a choice?" Adam asked. "These chains may be primitive but they're strong. We're not going to break out of here, so we need her help."

Sally peered through the gloom into the other cell. If Madeline Templeton heard them, she gave no sign of it. It was amazing how still she could sit. It was almost as if she were dead.

"She doesn't look like she can save herself," Sally said. "Never mind us."

"Remember Ann Templeton," Adam said. "Her real powers are hidden." He stopped and cleared his throat. "Hello? Madeline? Can you hear us?"

There was a long pause. Then, without moving or opening her eyes, the woman responded. Her voice was very soft and kind. She sounded like an angel. She also sounded cheerful, especially given her circumstances.

"I know who you are," she said. "I know you are from the future and I know how and why you have come into this time. Please don't be afraid of me, I will not harm you."

"We're not afraid of you," Adam said. "We know your great-great-great-great-granddaughter, Ann Templeton. We're friends of hers."

"I wouldn't go that far," Sally muttered.

"I know," the woman said quietly, still sitting with her eyes closed. "There is nothing to be concerned about."

"Excuse me," Sally said. "But we are all going to get fried when the sun rises. To me that is a big concern. I mean, I even hate to get a little sunburned."

"We were wondering," Adam said cautiously, "if perhaps you could use some of your magic to get us out of here?"

"No," Madeline Templeton said flatly. "That I cannot do."

Adam swallowed. "But if we don't get out of here we are doomed."

The witch held up a hand. "Silence. All will be well. Have faith."

"In you?" Sally asked sarcastically.

"Shh," Adam cautioned. "Don't make her mad. We need her."

"But she just said she won't help us," Sally complained.

"She didn't say that exactly. Let's wait and see what happens."

Sally began to panic. One of the few things that did scare her was fire. The thought of its spreading over her body was too much. She could just imagine what it would be like to have her skin peel off. Yuck!

"I don't want to wait," she said anxiously. "I know what's going to happen. Adam, look at the glow in the sky outside that window. It's almost dawn. They're going to come for us any minute!"

"Maybe the others can rescue us," Adam whispered.

"The others don't even know we're here!" Sally hissed.

"Because you didn't want them to know."

"I know that! Don't rub it in!"

Adam spoke with forced hope. "But it's possible that once they discover we're gone they'll come for us."

"But we'll be dead by then! Once we're dead they can't bring us back to life. Even if they can travel through time."

"I'm trying to be optimistic," Adam said.

"Optimism is only useful when you're safe and warm at home." Sally quieted down suddenly. They heard loud footsteps approaching. "They're coming for us! This is it! We're going to die!"

"Have faith, Sally," Adam pleaded, perhaps trying to convince himself as well as her. "We're going to be all right."

The men with the burning torches entered the prison.

The old ugly one with the black patch over his eye leered at them.

"What a beautiful day it is," he jeered. "A perfect day to watch three witches burn."

"We are not witches," Adam said defiantly.

The man thrust his torch through the bars. Adam tried to jump back but was not very successful with the chains on his hands and feet. He ended up getting brushed by the fire and let out a painful yelp.

"You sure cry like a witch," the man crooned.

"Leave him alone!" Sally screamed. "He's just a kid like me. And we've done nothing wrong. You should let us go."

The man acted sympathetic. "Oh, you're just poor children, I see. You're just like all the other children in this village."

"We are," Sally said. "We are no different."

The man hardened his stance. "Then where did you get those clothes? Where did you come from? And what was that evil device that you brought with you?"

"I got these clothes at JC Penney's," Sally said. "My mother bought them for me. And as far as where we came from—well, we fell out of a hot-air balloon."

"I don't think they have hot-air balloons here in these times," Adam whispered.

The ugly man gestured to his partners. "See, she speaks of devils! JC Penney's and hot balloon creatures that fly through the sky. We all know that only witches can fly. We have seen the pictures of them in our holy books. These two are as evil as this other witch. They must be destroyed with her if our town is to be made safe. Take them now and tie them to the wooden stakes outside. We will douse them with oil and set flames to their wicked forms!"

The men opened the door and walked toward them.

There was fire in their eyes but also fear.

"You're making a big mistake," Adam warned them.

His remark did not stop them. The three of them were dragged outside.

Even the great Madeline Templeton.

They dragged her by her long red hair. And she did nothing to stop them. Nothing.

All hope died inside Adam and Sally.

A surprisingly large crowd waited. They cheered when they saw the three witches.

"Burn them! Kill them! Witches!"

The stakes also waited. And the flames.

7

When the Time Toy was through with them, Cindy and Watch found themselves in a wonderful Spooksville where it seemed every building was made of glass and every path was lined with flowers and grass. They knew in an instant that they had not traveled back to the same time they had visited before.

"Where are we?" Cindy asked in awe.

"The question is *when* are we?" Watch corrected. "Look at the hills and the ocean. Once again the landscape is basically the same as in our time in Spooksville. So we know we are still in

Spooksville. But from the looks of things we have transported ourselves into the future."

"But you said the settings hadn't changed from when Sally and Adam used the thing?"

"I certainly didn't change them." Watch knelt beside the Time Toy, which had followed them into the future. He frowned as he studied the dials. "Everything seems to be the same as before. I don't know what went wrong."

Cindy sighed with delight as she looked around. "This looks like a great place. I wish we could explore it."

"We might as well explore it," Watch said. "We're not going anywhere just yet. Not until I figure out how to reset these controls to take us to where Sally and Adam went."

"But maybe they've come here," Cindy suggested.

"It's possible. Anything is possible."

While they were talking, a small boy in a shiny silver costume with long blue hair walked by. He had a pale face and wore a clear crystal around his neck. He paused and studied them and then nodded in approval.

"You are one of those who is trying to get the full experience," he said. "Frigid. I would have dressed up like the Heroes used to if I had thought of it."

"We are dressed the way we always dress," Cindy said.

The boy was momentarily puzzled.

"Are you guides here at the museum?" he asked. "I didn't know they had any. I thought the place was fully automated."

"Which museum are you talking about?" Watch asked. "Isn't this place still a city?"

"In a manner of speaking it is still a city," the boy replied. "It is Spooksville City. But the entire town was turned into a museum over a hundred years ago. Surely you must know that if you work here."

"We don't work here," Cindy said. "We are only here by accident."

"Where are you from then?" the boy asked.

Cindy and Watch exchanged glances.

"We are from Spooksville," Watch said carefully. "It is just that the last time we were here it looked . . . different."

The boy nodded. "They have updated the place. Have you seen the new Watch Center? They just opened it last month."

Cindy had to smile. "The Watch Center? What's there? I mean, why was it given that name?"

The boy was astounded. "But you must have heard of the great Watch. He was one of the original Heroes. Hundreds of files have been written about him. He was the inventor of antigravity that's used in all our modern jet craft and the Tachyon Pulse drive that we use to go to the planets. Everyone knows about Watch."

Watch seemed to be having trouble catching his breath.

"What were the names of the other original Heroes?" he stuttered.

"There was Adam Freeman, of course, the leader of the Heroes. And then there was Cindy Makey. Those were the most famous ones."

"What about Sally Wilcox?" Cindy asked with delight.

The boy's face darkened. "You must know that

history is not clear about Sara Wilcox. Some say she was one of the true Heroes and should be ranked with the others. But those people are in the minority. Most historians believe that she was responsible for many of the original group's problems. Some have even labeled her the Evil One."

Cindy giggled. "The historians are right. She was nothing but a troublemaker."

The boy also smiled but he continued to act confused. He offered his hand.

"My name is Tweek," he said. "What are your names?"

Watch and Cindy exchanged another long look.

"My name is Cindy," Cindy said finally. "And this is—well, his name is Watch."

Tweek shook their hands with enthusiasm. "Were you each named after the Heroes?" he asked.

"You could say that," Watch muttered.

"I am confused," Cindy said. "Why are these guys called the Heroes? I understand that Watch invented a bunch of stuff. But what about the others? What did they do that was so great?"

Tweek shook his head. "You guys really are new to this area. The Heroes are called the Heroes because they saved the earth countless times from destruction. They were the ones who kept the evil forces that operated in Spooksville from overwhelming the earth. They undertook this great task alone. No one in the world even knew what they were up against. But everyone knows that."

"Are there still evil forces in Spooksville?" Watch asked.

Tweek lowered his voice. "They say the Heroes purged them from this town but I have a sneaking suspicion that they are not all gone. Why, just the other day I thought I saw a ghost where the famous Evil House used to stand. What do you think of that?"

"Been there, done that," Cindy muttered.

Tweek continued to study them. "You know you guys look familiar. I could swear I've seen your faces before."

"In your history files, perhaps," Watch suggested.

"That's it!" Tweek explained. "You guys look

like the Heroes looked when they were young! Are you sure you're not in costume?"

Watch glanced around to make sure no one was watching them.

"Tweek," he said. "I have something extraordinary to tell you. At first you won't believe it but then it should make sense to you. I take it that you have studied the Heroes' memoirs?"

"Studied them? They're my favorite reading. I mean, frigid, they went on so many exciting adventures. Every kid has read about the Heroes. That's why I wanted to come here on my birthday."

"Is today your birthday, Tweek?" Cindy asked.

"Yeah. I was hatched twelve years ago."

Cindy frowned. "You were hatched?"

"Yeah. When were you hatched?"

"A long time ago," Watch said. "We're older than we look."

"Frigid! You are taking the new gene splices? I heard they work wonders."

"Not exactly," Watch continued. "You see, since you have read about the Heroes you must know that some of their adventures took place in other time zones. Like in other centuries and so on." Watch paused. "Did you read about that in your books?"

"Sure. The Heroes often had to enter other dimensions to keep the world safe."

"Exactly," Watch said. "They were all over the place, in time and space. And we're just like them. We're no different from them at all."

Tweek was having trouble keeping up. "How could you be like the Heroes? They were special. There has been no one like them in centuries."

"That's what Watch is trying to tell you," Cindy said. "We are from centuries ago. We *are* your famous Heroes. I am Cindy Makey. This is the great Watch."

Tweek stared at them in wonder. Then he began to laugh.

"I get it!" he said. "My father put you guys up to this. He wanted to surprise me on my birthday. Frigid! For a second there you guys had me convinced."

"This is not a prank," Watch said. "You are talking to two of the original Heroes. We came here by accident while searching for our friends, Sally and Adam."

Tweek quieted as if slapped. "That can't be true. You must be actors."

"No," Cindy said and pointed to the Time Toy, which remained in the middle of the path. "We are who we say we are. We used this device to travel through time. You must have read about it in our memoirs. I'm sure we would have written about it. This is the original Time Toy."

Tweek nodded reluctantly. "I have read about a device like this. But it was called the Time Terror by the real Cindy Makey."

"I am the real Cindy Makey," Cindy said. "But I can understand why I later called this thing the Time Terror. We've been having a terrible time since we ran into it."

Tweek was shaking his head. "No. This can't be true. This is too amazing. Not on my birthday, no."

"You can see that we resemble the Heroes," Watch said. "You can see that we have a device exactly like the one they wrote about. And you must know what that device was for—traveling through time. Beyond that I don't know how else we can prove ourselves to you. You just have to believe us, Tweek. Because we need your help."

Tweek was stunned. "But if you are the Heroes, how can I help you? You were all so powerful and brilliant."

"It's nice that history remembers us that way," Cindy said. "But the truth is that often while we fought the forces of evil, we were as scared as normal kids."

"We don't understand why we're in this time, in our future," Watch explained. "We were trying to go back in time to where we believe our friends are right now. But we ended up here."

"But it's possible that our friends are here right now," Cindy added. "Have you seen any other funny characters besides us?"

"No," Tweek said, still grappling with what they were saying. "You are the funniest characters I have ever met."

"We're your Heroes," Watch said firmly. "But we don't have time to argue with you. In your history files, does it explain how this Time Terror works? Why one time it sent your Heroes backward in time and why another time it sent them forward in time?"

"Of course," Tweek said. "Everyone knows about the Time Terror. When you go to use it, if you touch the right bolt on its neck first, then you go back in time. But if you touch the left bolt first, you go forward in time. It's common knowledge. I can take you to the Time Terror exhibit if you would like. The device is on display there."

"Sorry, but we'll have to do that later," Cindy said.

"Much later," Watch agreed. "But thank you, Tweek. I think I know now what I did wrong. I should be able to correct my mistake."

"Wait a second," Tweek said. "You guys are serious? You really are two of the Heroes?"

"We can only tell you so many times," Cindy said as Watch knelt to readjust the Time Terror.

"And you are going to transport yourselves off to another time right now?" Tweek asked.

"In less than a minute," Watch muttered as he readjusted the dial on the top of the device, as well as the arms on the belly clock. Tweek clenched his fists in excitement.

"This is too good to be true!" he shouted at the sky. "Oh, please, let me go with you."

Cindy shook her head. "Sorry, Tweek, we can't mess up the time line any more than it has already been messed up."

"Yeah," Watch said. "Damage has already been done. We don't even know if we are still who we used to be. We may even have lost a friend for good."

"Who?" Tweek asked.

"That's the problem," Cindy said. "We don't know him anymore. He's no longer a part of our past, if he ever did exist."

Tweek stared in wonder. "Frigid. This is so wonderful! But you have to take me with you. I promise I'll do everything you say. I won't even speak to anyone unless you say I can. Please, it's my birthday and there would be nothing more exciting for me in the whole world than to share an adventure with the Heroes."

Cindy glanced at Watch. "What do you think?"

Watch sighed. "It just increases the risk."

"But Tweek was able to help us already," Cindy

said. "Who knows? He might be able to help us again."

"That's true," Watch said.

Tweek held up his hand. "I swear on the great memories of the original Heroes that I will not cause you any trouble."

Cindy pulled down his hand. "Please don't swear on our names. It makes us uncomfortable."

Watch straightened. "If you're coming with us then you'd better stand beside us, Tweek. This thing will be humming and shining in just a few seconds."

Tweek was in ecstasy. "This is the greatest birthday a guy could have."

"Let's just hope you live to see your next birthday," Watch muttered.

There was a flash of brilliant light.

There were stars everywhere.

Once more they left Spooksville for Spooksville.

8

Adam and Sally's situation had gone from bad to worse. They had been tied to wooden stakes down at the beach. Oil was being poured all over the kindling wood at their feet. Off to their left Madeline Templeton seemed to be in another of her trances. She had her eyes closed and could have been communing with an alien on Mars for all she seemed to care about her predicament.

In front of them the crowd continued to jeer. There were even kids present. Their rosy faces smiled up at them with perverse anticipation. Apparently public executions were a form of entertainment. The oil was almost distributed. Soon men with torches would step forward and the agony would begin.

"I'm scared," Sally whispered on Adam's left. "I don't want to die this way."

"I would prefer not to die any way," Adam replied. "I'm only twelve years old."

Sally looked in the direction of Madeline Templeton.

"Why doesn't she do anything to save herself at least?" she wondered aloud.

"I don't understand what she's waiting for," Adam agreed. Yet something nagged at him about the situation, besides the obvious. "Sally, do you remember the first day I met you? The day I moved here?"

Sally trembled as she eyed the waiting torches.

"Of course," she said. "But this is hardly a good time to reminisce, Adam."

"But you told me something about this time. About this very day. Watch was there as well. We were trying to figure out how the Secret Path worked. We were trying to visit the spot of each major event in Madeline Templeton's life. This spot, this day, was one of them. I remember Watch said, 'After the reservoir, we go back to the beach. That's where the townsfolk tried to burn her alive for being a witch—the first time.'"

Sally showed interest. "I remember."

"Then I said, 'What do you mean they *tried* to burn her?'"

Sally nodded vigorously. "And I said, 'The wood they stacked up around her refused to catch on fire. And snakes crawled out of it and killed the judge who condemned her to death.'" Sally paused and tried to catch her breath. The noise of the crowd was nerve-racking, as was the smell of the oil. "But, Adam, that might not be today. This might be the second time they tried to burn her to death."

"Did they succeed the second time?" Adam asked.

"I think so. But I'm not sure."

"I wish you knew for sure," Adam said.

Sally began to pant. The oil was all in place. It swam in the wood at their feet. Men with torches stepped forward.

"It's hard to remember stuff right now," Sally moaned. "Oh no. This is really it. And I thought we were special, that we would never die. I don't understand why they won't let us repent or something. Where is the town priest? They have a church for goodness sake. I'll confess all my sins. I'll do anything they want if they'll just let us go. Adam! Make them stop!"

"We're not witches!" Adam yelled. "We're just kids lost in time!"

The old man with the eye patch laughed out loud.

"Now they admit to fooling with time itself!" he yelled back. "Witches! All of them! Light the wood! Let them burn!"

"Burn!" the crowd chanted.

The torches touched the oil.

It ignited immediately. The flames began to lick over the wood. Within a few seconds the heat and smoke was extraordinary. Adam and Sally twisted their heads from side to side to escape it, but there was no escape.

"Adam!" Sally cried. "It hurts!"

"Have faith!" Adam cried back, even though he had lost all hope. In his worst nightmares he could not have imagined an end worse than this. It didn't seem fair that after all he had gone through, after all he had achieved in his short life, it should end like this. He supposed a part of him was still hoping for a miracle.

Then there was a miracle of sorts.

At least the beginning of one.

How it would all turn out, time would tell.

A roar suddenly went through the crowd, but it wasn't because of the burnings. A woman had come screaming from a side street. She was terror stricken.

"There are more witches in Springville!" she shouted. "They are up the road! I saw them! A girl witch and two boy witches! One of them wears a cloak of silver! They have brought the tiny demon with them! Please come and help!"

Burnings at the stake were fun, but Adam guessed witches running around town were even more exciting. As a whole the crowd flooded in the direction the frightened woman was gesturing. In seconds they had vanished, although they could be heard yelling and cursing behind the buildings. Incredibly Adam and Sally were left alone with the old man with the eye patch and two guards. Not to mention Madeline Templeton.

Finally the witch opened her eyes.

The flames grew higher, the smoke thicker.

She showed no fear. She smiled at the old man.

He was obviously the judge.

The one who had condemned her to death.

He trembled under her gaze, seeing how the crowd had deserted him. The other two guards instinctively backed up. Madeline Templeton continued to grin.

"You think you finally have me," she said in her gentle voice. "You did not know that I have more powers than can be found in all this world. That I have allies that can reach to aid me from even a distant time. And you did not know that I had a small knife hidden in my shoe."

With that last remark the witch held up her freed hands.

She had already cut her ropes.

Possibly the moment she had been tied.

The old judge stepped back and drew a sword.

"You will not escape your just punishment," he swore.

The witch laughed. "It is you who will not escape me."

Madeline Templeton stepped down from the funeral pyre.

"Excuse me?" Adam said. "Ms. Templeton? I don't mean to bother you at a time like this but my friend and I have a little problem here. These flames are getting higher and I think we are about to be burned to death. I was wondering if you could use your knife to cut our ropes as well. If you could, we would really appreciate it."

Sally nodded strongly, her face dripping sweat.

"I would, too," Sally said. "Really, truly."

Madeline Templeton seemed pleased. She spoke to Adam.

"You show great faith. I can see why my ancestor speaks highly of you. I will do as you ask and release you and your friend. But I must warn you that your trials are not over. As you can see this is a very unusual day."

"As long as we're not on fire I think we can

handle what happens next," Adam said. He didn't really want to have a lengthy conversation with the woman. Yet once she had made up her mind she moved quickly. As deft as a cat she leaped back up on the funeral pyre. She took care of Sally's ropes first, which was fine with Sally. But Adam was free seconds later. He had to help Sally down from the stacked wood, around the spreading flames. She was close to fainting.

Perhaps the judge saw that. He had struck them as someone who liked to pick on the helpless. Rather than charging Madeline Templeton with his saber, he made a stab at Sally. Adam was dizzy and saw the thrust a second too late. Fortunately the witch was more alert. As the evil judge bore down on Sally, Madeline stepped in front of him and tripped him. His deadly thrust went wide.

No. It found a mark.

The judge landed on his own sword.

It impaled him. Suddenly there was blood everywhere.

Neither Adam nor Sally had ever seen anyone die.

They were sickened deep inside.

In all their adventures things had always turned out all right in the end.

It did not matter that this man was trying to kill them.

The other guards turned and ran.

The witch stared down at the body as it lay on the ground.

"So Judge Jeff Poole gets his just rewards," she said, but there was no joy in her voice. She glanced at them. "Do you know what this means?" she asked.

"Poole?" Adam muttered, still trying to catch his breath. "That is the last name of our friend, Bryce."

"Was this his great-great-great-great-great-grandfather?" Sally asked, tears on her face. The witch nodded solemnly.

"It was he," she said.

"But then that means Bryce no longer exists in the future?" Adam said.

"His whole family line has been wiped out," Madeline Templeton agreed.

Adam was shocked. "This is terrible."

"But there are worse things," Sally said quickly.

Adam glared at her. "How can you say that? He's our friend."

"He was your friend," the witch said softly, before turning her gaze in the direction of her castle, which stood on its hill. "He is no more. But I cannot help you with that problem. It is your responsibility. Right now I must retreat to my castle and bring out my defenses."

"Can we come with you?" Sally begged.

The witch gave her a sad smile. "You have to ask yourself who created the diversion that allowed us all to escape."

"Watch and Cindy?" Adam gasped.

"Yes," the witch said.

"But the woman said there were three witches," Sally said. "Bryce must be with them. He must be all right."

"Things are not always as they appear," Madeline Templeton said as she turned away. "You must excuse me, children. My battle has only begun."

When she was gone, Sally said, "What should we do now?"

"We have to find the Time Toy," Adam said.

"But Cindy and Watch must have it, if they're here."

"No. I think they've brought their own. Otherwise they couldn't have got here. Ours must still be here, probably back at the prison where we were held captive all night."

"But it sounds like Watch and Cindy are about to be taken captive," Sally said. "Shouldn't we rescue them first?"

"No. We can't do anything for them with this angry mob running around," Adam said. "We need a weapon. We have to return to the future."

"But what are you going to do?" Sally asked.

They could hear the cries coming from the other side of the buildings. It sounded as if the angry mob had finally caught its prey. There was a loud sound of celebration. Adam stared in their direction and spoke grimly.

"You'll see," he said.

9

Adam and Sally did find their Time Toy where they thought it would be, in a room adjoining the prison cells. The guards were out. Quickly Adam reset the dials and turned the device on. Sally held his hand as the hum peaked and the light flashed.

They flew through the cosmos.

They seemed to fly forever.

But when they came to a halt and looked around they weren't where they were supposed to be. The ocean and the hills were pretty much the same but now there wasn't even a sign of the town. Sally gasped.

"Could something we did in the past have wiped out our entire future?" she asked.

Adam was puzzled. "This makes no sense."

"Yes, it does. I'm always kidding Bryce about how he thinks he keeps saving the world but maybe he has saved the world once or twice. And if we just wiped out his family line, then maybe we wiped out humanity as well."

Adam shook his head. "I refuse to accept that Bryce is that important to all of history. I must have made a mistake with the Time Toy."

"But you said you watched what Watch did?"

"No, I didn't. *You* said you watched what he did. I hardly noticed." Adam knelt beside the device. "It is possible there are more adjustments required than meet the eye. Let me fiddle with it some more. But don't move from my side. If I suddenly vanish, you might be trapped here with no way of going anywhere."

"Don't worry. I'm not in the mood for a walk." She put a hand on Adam's shoulder as he worked. "Thanks for helping me face the fire. Honestly, I've never been so scared in my life. I saw no way of getting out of that one. But somehow you kept your faith."

"Don't flatter me. I was ready to throw in the towel as well."

"Then you're an expert when it comes to faking courage."

"It comes in handy in this town," Adam muttered.

Sally shivered in the cold wind.

"I just hope Watch and Cindy aren't burning right now," she said.

Adam suddenly stood. "No, I don't think they are. In fact, I don't think they are going to burn in the next two hundred years."

Sally was astounded. "We're still in the past?"

"We are even deeper in the past. I think I realize my mistake. I touched the neck bolts in a different sequence than I did before. I am pretty sure that I know now how to get us back to our present time."

"Are you going to take us back right after we left?" she asked.

"No. I want to return to Spooksville a couple of months *before* we left. Remember that hand laser we had? The one Ann Templeton took from us Halloween night. She thought kids like us should not be playing with such exotic weapons. I want to go back and get it out of my bedroom."

"That might be dangerous. You might run into yourself. The universe might explode."

"It's less dangerous than returning to the Spooksville witch trials without anything to defend ourselves. Those people are so superstitious, there's no reasoning with them. Once I have the laser I can set it to stun and drive the crowd away and rescue Watch and Cindy."

"But what are we going to do for Bryce?" Sally asked.

"I thought you didn't care about him."

"I care, of course I do. I just act like I don't care."

"Why do you do that?" Adam asked.

"I enjoy being tough. It's part of my carefully cultivated image."

"I should have known." Adam pulled her closer. "Get ready, I'm going to activate the device. If my calculations are correct, we should appear in Spooksville the day before Halloween."

"And if they're wrong we'll get eaten by a dinosaur or else materialize inside a rock," Sally said. "Really, Adam, I don't know why I let you take me places this way."

Adam laughed and turned on the Time Toy.

"Because it's the only way to fly," he said.

10

Tweek clearly regretted having begged to spend his birthday with the two great Heroes from the past. Along with Cindy and Watch, he was standing tied to a wooden stake on Spooksville's beach. The earlier pile of wood had already burned off but that was not a problem for the industrious townsfolk. There was more where that had come from, as well as more oil. The people were in a fierce mood. The death of their judge had sent them into a frenzy. They were talking about storming the castle next.

Apparently Madeline Templeton had gotten away again.

"Do you think Sally and Adam burned here?" Cindy cried. She was in the middle, between Tweek and Watch.

"I hope not," Watch said. "I hope they're about to rescue us. Hey, Tweek, do we get rescued or not?"

Tweek was a mass of pain and sorrow.

"I don't know," he moaned. "I never read a file that talked about this. I don't want to die! Save me!"

"We don't want to destroy your illusions about us," Watch said. "But we're not super-human beings. We generally rely on our courage, wits, and a good dose of good luck. But we may have run out of all three today."

"Why didn't we come back in time before them?" Cindy asked. "That was your intention, wasn't it?"

"Yeah," Watch admitted. "But I think I set the watch hands just a little off."

"It happens," Cindy said. "Don't blame yourself."

"I blame him," Tweek cried as he eyed the men approaching with the burning torches. "I can't die back in time. Today is my birthday."

"I don't think they would be impressed by that fact," Watch muttered.

Tweek's face was a thousand tears. "But I'm so young. I only hatched twelve years ago."

"You don't want to talk to them about hatching," Cindy advised. "They'll really think you're a witch."

"Not that they haven't already made up their minds on that point," Watch said.

The men with the torches lit the oil.

The burning wood began to smoke and crack.

The crowd shouted its pleasure.

Cindy closed her eyes and cried out. "It's not over, Watch! It can't be over! You have to live and do all those great things you're supposed to do! I have to live and see you do them! Watch!"

"We will be victorious!" Watch yelled back.

Suddenly the shouts of pleasure from the crowd turned to terror.

Cindy opened her eyes to see red darts of flame

splashing into the crowd. At first she thought it was a hallucination, a product of the heat searing her face. But the crowd was definitely attempting to flee the area. What was even more amazing was when Cindy heard Sally speak to her. Cindy glanced over her shoulder and saw Sally cutting her ropes.

"Hi, girl," Sally said. "This getting burned at the stake routine is pretty intense, don't you think?"

Cindy grinned with relief. "I knew you'd save me."

Sally hacked through the ropes. "Me in particular?"

"Yes. Only you would have the nerve to save anyone from these flames."

"Why, thank you. I take that as a compliment."

"I meant it that way," Cindy said as her hands were finally freed. Just in time, the flames were only inches away. Sally knelt and worked quickly on her feet. She gestured to the side.

"Who is the shiny guy in the silver suit?" Sally asked.

"His name is Tweek. He's from the future."

"Should I try to save him?"

"Of course. It's his birthday today."

The flames were getting worse. The smoke was choking.

Sally coughed. "I'll cut him free—after Watch."

Cindy's feet were freed. She stepped in Tweek's direction, balancing on the unsteady logs beneath her feet.

"Don't worry, I'll set you free," Cindy said to Tweek. "Where's Adam?" she asked Sally.

"He's the one with the laser pistol shooting down the rain of red fire. He said it would work and he was right. This crowd is terrified. I bet they've had their fill of witches for today." Sally paused. "You haven't seen Bryce anywhere, have you?"

Tweek had already fainted, or else he was acting like he was unconscious. Cindy knelt behind his stake and began to tug at his ropes.

"Who?" Cindy asked.

"Bryce," Sally said as she started to free Watch.

"We don't know any Bryce," Watch said.

Sally snickered as she began to cut into his ropes.

"Sure," she said. "Bryce is one of us. I mean, it's true that we just accidentally killed his great-great-great-great-great-grandfather. But that's no reason you should have forgotten him so soon."

Watch choked on the smoke. "I honestly have never heard of anyone named Bryce in my life."

"I've never heard the name either," Cindy called over. Tweek was showing signs of life. Definite signs.

"I'm being rescued!" he cried. "My Heroes!"

"It's Sally who has rescued us," Cindy said.

Tweek lost his excited grin.

"The Evil One?" he asked.

"What's that you called me?" Sally called over.

"It's nothing," Cindy muttered.

Sally shook her head. "I just don't understand how you guys could have forgotten Bryce while I still remember him."

"If this person you are talking about did once

exist," Watch said, "then you were back here in this time when he was destroyed in our future time. Your memory of him was not erased at that instant, but ours was."

"What was he like?" Cindy called over.

"He was handsome," Sally said. "You were in love with him, Cindy."

Cindy appeared stunned. She even paused while freeing Tweek.

"That's impossible," she said. "I love . . ." She didn't finish.

Sally giggled. "You told me once that the only boy you could ever love was Bryce. He meant that much to you."

"Please keep loosening my ropes," Tweek told Cindy.

"Sorry," Cindy muttered as she returned to the task. She had to hurry in to get him free. The flames were licking his silver shoes. Fortunately they seemed fire resistant. But Sally's remarks had upset her. It was Adam she cared about. Who was this other one?

Sally moved up beside her, her knife at the ready. Sally was already through with Watch. He was climbing down from the burning logs, trying to catch his breath. But Sally paused as she cut through Tweek's ropes and stared at Cindy's hair. The kid from the future was getting just a little impatient.

"My toes are hot!" he cried. "They hurt and it's my birthday."

"Shh," Sally said. "Cindy, you have red hair."

"So? I have always had red hair."

"No. You're a blond."

"You're lying! My red hair is my most stunning feature. You have always been jealous of it." Cindy was distraught. "I don't know if I can believe anything you say."

Sally spoke seriously. "I lied to you about Bryce. He really did exist but you were not in love with him. I was just teasing you, and I'm sorry, I shouldn't have done that. But you really are a blond, Cindy. You have very beautiful blond hair. Usually."

"And I suppose my eyes are blue instead of green?"

Sally peered closer and then frowned. "Yeah.

They are supposed to be blue. What happened to them?"

Cindy shook her head and coughed.

She began to climb off the burning logs.

"We will have to sort this out later," she said. "I'm getting a headache thinking about all this time travel."

11

The five of them ended up in the witch's castle. In her dining room. It was the only place they felt safe in town, and it wasn't really all that safe. The crowd was recovering from Adam's laser blasts. They were gathering outside and it seemed only a matter of time before they attacked the castle. Yet Madeline Templeton seemed unperturbed. She was off with her trolls, planning defensive strategy. She had told them once again that she was not going to help them with their problems, although she had said nothing about kicking them out. They were grateful for the relative safety of her castle so they could catch their breath.

"Our priority must be to save Bryce," Adam said as he paced in front of them and the Time Toy or the Time Terror. They were using both names, depending on who was speaking at the moment.

They had in their possession the one Adam and Sally had brought back through time. Like a menacing statue, it sat on the floor and waited for them to tilt the sands of time one more time. Adam had been careful not to leave it for the angry crowd but Cindy and Watch had lost theirs to the mob. That is, if there ever were two of the weird devices in any single time frame.

But that was a question they didn't care to ponder right then.

"It's hard for Cindy and me to make Bryce a priority when we don't even know him," Watch said.

"But you will know him if we save him," Adam said. "You'll like him, too. Trust me, Watch, you'll think he was worth sacrificing for."

"I trust you," Watch said.

"Am I really blond?" Cindy blurted out.

Adam paused and stared at her. He frowned.

"What happened to your hair?" he asked.

Cindy buried her face in her lap. "Never mind!"

"From what you and Sally have said," Watch said to Adam, "Bryce Poole ceased to exist because Judge Jeff Poole was slain when he tried to kill Sally. That is the main moment that has been distorted." He glanced at Cindy. "Although obviously other little things have been distorted as well."

"Hey, Watch," Sally said. "Where are your glasses? How can you see without them?"

Adam grimaced. "Sally. Maybe we shouldn't ask these questions. They obviously don't remember certain things."

"I have never worn glasses," Watch said.

"You are missing your four watches as well," Sally muttered.

"Why would I wear four watches?" Watch asked.

"Never mind," Adam said. "Somehow we must go back in time to prevent Judge Poole from dying."

"I don't know if I like that idea," Sally said. "If he doesn't die then I die."

Tweek nodded to himself in the corner. "The Evil One."

"What is this Evil One business?" Sally demanded.

Cindy looked up and color returned to her cheeks. "In the future we visited we are all seen as great Heroes. History worships us. In fact, they have turned all of Spooksville into a museum in our honor. There is even a special Watch Center to honor all the great things Watch is going to invent when he gets older."

"It is a frigid building," Tweek exclaimed.

"What is this *frigid* business?" Sally asked.

"It's his way of saying *cool*," Watch said.

Sally was interested. "So in the future we're all considered real frigid?"

Cindy giggled. She was enjoying the revenge.

"Not you," she said. "Many historians have labeled you the Evil One."

Sally's face dropped. "But what did I do wrong? Tweek? Tell me the truth or I'll throw you outside to that angry mob."

Tweek nodded. "It is true what Cindy says. Only a few historians see you as a force for good."

Sally jumped up. "But what did I do wrong? Specifically?"

Tweek was uneasy. "You are remembered as the one who tormented the other Heroes. Particularly Cindy Makey."

Sally was furious. "I bet it is Cindy Makey's personal diary that gives your stupid historians these stupid beliefs!"

Tweek nodded. "Cindy's diaries did play an important role in the reconstruction of what went on in early Spooksville."

Sally was beside herself. "I can't believe this. Here I risk life and limb to rescue you guys from all the miserable predicaments you get into and then I am trashed in the history books."

"It is said you got the group into many of their worst situations," Tweek said reluctantly. He seemed a little afraid of Sally. She pounced on him with that remark.

"Name one situation!" she said. "I dare you."

"This situation seems to fit the bill nicely," Watch muttered.

"You were the one who used the Time Toy when we told you not to," Cindy added. "None of us even wanted to touch the thing."

"And you insisted we take the Wishing Stone home," Watch added.

Tweek brightened. "And you led your friends into the demonic realm on the other side of the Secret Path."

Sally turned away in disgust. "How does he know that?"

Adam held up his hand. "We don't have time for this. We have to save Bryce. We have to come up with a plan. We can't sit in here forever. For all we know this mob kills Madeline today. We know they got to her eventually. Watch, you have pinpointed the crucial moment. It's when Judge Poole tries to kill Sally. If Sally hadn't come back in time, he wouldn't have tried to kill her. And then Madeline wouldn't have tripped him. And he wouldn't have died."

"That's correct," Watch said. "It all fits together."

Adam nodded. "Good. Then let us focus on how

we can alter that moment without wrecking the entire time line. Any ideas?"

"We have the hand laser," Cindy said. "What if you go back in time, Adam, and stun Judge Poole from behind before he can charge Sally?"

"He might still fall on his blade," Sally warned.

"It's unlikely," Adam said, glancing over his shoulder. "Madeline Templeton tripped him in such a way that he almost had to fall on it."

"Are you saying she killed him on purpose?" Cindy asked.

"Yes," Sally said. "He was the one who condemned her to death, so I can kind of understand her wanting to kill him." She paused, remembering the moment. "I like Cindy's plan. It's simple and clean."

"But then there'll be two Adams in the same time frame," Watch warned. "What if they run into each other? We've discussed this before—I think. We don't know what would happen, do we? Maybe I should be the one to try to stun the judge."

"But you couldn't hit a wall if you were standing right in front of it," Sally said.

Watch didn't agree. "I'm an excellent shot."

"At this moment you may be a good shot," Adam said. "But the moment you stun Judge Poole many changes to the time line should reverse themselves. You could be standing there blind as a bat without your glasses. You wouldn't even be able to set the Time Toy to return to this time right here."

"But my glasses should reappear if I am supposed to be wearing them," Watch said.

"Unless you lost them earlier in this adventure," Sally said. "With all that's happened today they could have fallen off a dozen times."

Watch nodded reluctantly. "That's a good point. But maybe we should send Tweek back in time to that moment. He's from the future. He should know how to use a laser pistol. Also, he wasn't present at that time. There's no danger that he could run into himself."

But Tweek looked worried. "I love to read about you Heroes. But I never wanted to be like you."

"That's not what you said when we were in the future Spooksville," Cindy said.

Tweek lowered his head. "I went through

enough stress when they tried to burn me at the stake. It's my birthday, I'm supposed to be having fun."

"Being a hero is not always a joyride," Sally said bitterly. "Even if history doesn't thank you for it."

"Let's not get off track," Adam said. "It's decided then. I'll return in time to just before Judge Poole tries to kill Sally. I'll take up a position behind him and stun him. I doubt Madeline Templeton will try to harm him if he is lying helpless on the ground. Then I will come back here and everything should be frigid, I mean, cool. Then we can return to our own time."

"And I can go home?" Tweek asked.

"Yes," Adam said. "You can go back to where you belong."

"You have to time your return to right now perfectly," Watch warned. "Set it an hour from now if you must. Better to error on the side of too late than too early. I don't want to see two of you in this room."

"I've already thought of that," Adam said as he checked his laser pistol and then tucked it in his belt. He knelt and readjusted the Time Toy.

Watch helped him. It was tricky trying to estimate when Judge Poole had died. Finally the guys were satisfied with the adjustments. Everyone wished Adam good luck.

"When I return Bryce should be here," Adam said.

"Is that true?" Cindy asked.

"Yes," Watch said. "If he had not vanished from when we were in Sally's garage—which is when I think he must have vanished—then Bryce should have gone with us into the future. And then back with us to this time."

"But we have no record of Bryce in our future," Tweek said.

"Because by the time Watch and Cindy arrived in your future Bryce's family tree had already been wiped out," Adam explained. He leaned over and touched the bolts on the neck of the device. "You guys should get in the other room before it gets warmed up. I don't know how wide its teleporting beam is."

"Good idea," Watch said as the rest of them hurried out of the room. But Watch paused in the doorway to wish Adam good luck once more.

Watch added, "Don't miss. If you shoot yourself or Sally I can't imagine what will happen."

Adam nodded. "It'll take me just one shot. See you later."

Watch nodded. "Ain't that the truth."

Watch left the room.

Adam sighed and tried to quiet his pounding heart.

The Time Toy hummed. The Time Terror glowed.

Adam stared at it and wondered if he was staring at his own death.

There was a flash of light. Adam was gone.

12

An hour later, when the gang was back in the witch's dining room and the mob outside was trying to storm the castle walls, Adam reappeared at exactly the same moment Bryce did. Only Bryce was now tall and blond and had a wild look in his eyes. This bothered only Adam and Sally because the others still didn't remember what he was supposed to be like. This new version of Bryce waved his hand stupidly at them.

"Hi ya, guys," he mumbled. "Want to play Frisbee?"

Sally groaned. "Now he's a moron." She glanced at Cindy. "At least you're a blond again."

Cindy frowned. "I have always been a blond. What is it with you?"

Sally lowered her head. "I'm not saying anything anymore."

Watch came over and offered Bryce his hand.

"Pleased to meet you, Bryce," Watch said. "I've heard so much about you."

Bryce just stared stupidly at Watch's outstretched hand.

"Do you like pinball?" Bryce asked with slurred speech.

Watch glanced at Adam. "I take it this is not the Bryce you remember?"

Adam sighed and turned aside. "I don't know what went wrong. I stunned Judge Poole. He went down. I stayed long enough to see that Madeline Templeton didn't harm him. Everything should be back the way it was. *Bryce* should be back the way he was."

Watch considered. "Perhaps when you shot him with the laser you affected him in a subtle genetic way. Who knows what laser fire does to DNA anyway? The judge was old but he still must have had a child after today. Perhaps the genetic damage was passed on to that child and Bryce's entire family tree was weakened. That's why he is not who he used to be."

"Do you have a toy truck?" Bryce asked Tweek.

"Ah. No," Tweek said, looking worried. His Heroes were having problems. He was probably wondering if he would ever get home.

Adam pounded the stone wall in frustration. Outside the shouts of the mob were getting louder, although it sounded like the witch was fighting back. They heard loud explosions and could smell gunpowder.

"This entire situation is impossible to fix," Adam said. "Even if we do get Bryce back the way he was—which I don't think we can—then we still have all the other minor distortions. Cindy will have green hair next."

"Don't say that, Adam," Cindy snapped.

Watch nodded. "We can't go back and try to fix the past. There are too many variables. We have changed things in too many places. The more we try to repair the past, the more we mess it up."

Adam looked beaten. "Then it's hopeless? The world we knew can never be reclaimed? The people we loved can never be returned to us?"

It was Watch's turn to smile.

"There's always hope," he said. "But we have been looking for it in the wrong place. We have tried to fix the past by going into the past."

"But there's no other way," Adam protested.

"Of course there is," Watch said. "The answer is so obvious that none of us has been able to see it. We can only heal the past by going into the future. I will take the Time Toy. I will go alone, to the night we found the Time Toy in the alleyway after the movie. I will simply take it away. None of you will see it when you come out of the theater. It will be as if none of these trips through time ever happened. Then, finally, everything will be as it was supposed to be."

Bryce began to lick his palms. "I like eggs," he said.

Tweek groaned. "Oh no."

Adam faced Watch and stared deep into his eyes. "But you realize what you are saying?" he told his friend. "Everything will be exactly the way it was for all of us except you. There will then be two of you in that time."

"Don't worry," Watch said. "I'll be careful. I'll never run into myself."

"But what will the other Watch do?" Cindy asked, concerned. "How will he live?"

Watch smiled faintly. "You are really asking how I will live. I have thought about that and I believe I'll be OK. I mean, I'll get to do all the things my counterpart can't do living in Spooksville. I can travel the world."

"But you can never see us again," Adam said.

Watch nodded sadly. "But at least I'll know that one of me is with you guys. That he's not lonely."

"You'll be lonely," Cindy said. "You can't do this."

"She is right," Adam said. "I should be the one to remove the Time Toy from the alley."

Watch shook his head. "I am used to being alone. Besides, I have to do it. The idea was mine."

"But we'll worry about you," Sally said.

"But you won't," Watch said. "You won't re-member that any of this has happened because it won't have happened—for you. You'll leave the movie theater and go home as if nothing were the matter. That's the way it should be." He lowered his head. "Only I will remember. The part of me that's here right now."

Adam put his hand on Watch's shoulder.

"It's a brilliant plan, a brave plan," he said. "I wish I could help you with it."

Watch smiled and wiped away an unexpected tear. He looked at all of them with great affection. They had never seen so much feeling on his face, although they had always known it was deep inside him. But he had nothing to hide now. He spoke with great passion.

"You can help me by being happy. By helping the other Watch to be happy."

They promised they would do that for him.

Epilogue

After the film, they exited through the rear doorway into the alleyway. There was a commotion going on in the lobby and they didn't want to get involved. It sounded as if the vampire woman was trying to drink the blood of a young couple. Sometimes in Spooksville it was better to stay out of other people's business. Even Adam, who loved to save everyone from harm, was finally learning that.

For some reason they paused in the alleyway.

Together they glanced to their right.

It was as if they expected to see something.

Hidden in the shadows.

But, of course, there was nothing there.

As a group they burst out laughing.

"That movie must have scared us more than we realized," Sally said.

"Yeah," Cindy agreed. "I half expected to see one of those alien monsters waiting there, ready to jump us."

"It just shows that we can still be scared by a good movie," Adam said.

"Aren't you glad we talked you into it?" Bryce asked.

"Yeah," Adam admitted. "I love to be scared."

"But I've had enough chills and thrills for one night," Cindy said. "Let's get home."

They headed out of the alleyway. But then they noticed Watch was lagging behind, still staring at that spot in the alley where they had all looked.

"Hey, Watch," Sally called. "What's bothering you?"

Watch quickened his pace and caught up with them.

He looked pale and seemed to be shivering.

"That's so weird," he said. "I just had the

strangest feeling. I can't explain it, but I have goose bumps all over me. It was like déjà vu and a waking dream meshed together."

Sally laughed. "When you get a chill like that it means someone just walked over your grave."

"That's an old wives' tale," Adam said.

"A lot of them are true," Sally said, taking Watch's arm. "Come, I'll personally make you a big cup of hot chocolate, Watch. We'll drive away those nasty chills."

The gang walked off together, laughing in the night. None of them noticed the young man standing in the shadows of the alleyway, staring at the gang as they left. None of them heard the single word he uttered before he, too, turned away and disappeared into the night.

"Goodbye," he said.

About the Author

Little is known about Christopher Pike, although he is supposed to be a strange man. It is rumored that he was born in New York but grew up in Los Angeles. He has been seen in Santa Barbara lately, so he probably lives there now. But no one really knows what he looks like, or how old he is. It is possible that he is not a real person, but an eccentric creature visiting from another world. When he is not writing, he sits and stares at the walls of his huge haunted house. A short, ugly troll wanders around him in the dark and whispers scary stories in his ear.

Christopher Pike is one of this planet's best-selling authors of young adult fiction.

LOOK FOR THE NEXT

SPOOKSVILLE #17

THE THING IN THE CLOSET

by

Christopher Pike

COMING IN MID-JUNE 1997

From Minstrel® Books
Published by Pocket Books

SPOOKSVILLE

BY CHRISTOPHER PIKE

Available from Minstrel® Books
Published by Pocket Books

R·L·STINE'S GHOSTS OF FEAR STREET®

1 HIDE AND SHRIEK 52941-2/$3.99
2 WHO'S BEEN SLEEPING IN MY GRAVE? 52942-0/$3.99
3 THE ATTACK OF THE AQUA APES 52943-9/$3.99
4 NIGHTMARE IN 3-D 52944-7/$3.99
5 STAY AWAY FROM THE TREE HOUSE 52945-5/$3.99
6 EYE OF THE FORTUNETELLER 52946-3/$3.99
7 FRIGHT KNIGHT 52947-1/$3.99
8 THE OOZE 52948-X/$3.99
9 REVENGE OF THE SHADOW PEOPLE 52949-8/$3.99
10 THE BUGMAN LIVES! 52950-1/$3.99
11 THE BOY WHO ATE FEAR STREET 00183-3/$3.99
12 NIGHT OF THE WERECAT 00184-1/$3.99
13 HOW TO BE A VAMPIRE 00185-X/$3.99
14 BODY SWITCHERS FROM OUTER SPACE 00186-8/$3.99
15 FRIGHT CHRISTMAS 00187-6/$3.99
16 DON'T EVER GET SICK AT GRANNY'S 00188-4/$3.99
17 HOUSE OF A THOUSAND SCREAMS 00190-6/$3.99
18 CAMP FEAR GHOULS 00191-4/$3.99
19 THREE EVIL WISHES 00189-2/$3.99
20 SPELL OF THE SCREAMING JOKERS 00192-2/$3.99

Available from Minstrel® Books
Published by Pocket Books

POCKET
B O O K S

Simon & Schuster Mail Order Dept. BWB
200 Old Tappan Rd., Old Tappan, N.J. 07675

Please send me the books I have checked above. I am enclosing $_____(please add $0.75 to cover the postage and handling for each order. Please add appropriate sales tax). Send check or money order--no cash or C.O.D.'s please. Allow up to six weeks for delivery. For purchase over $10.00 you may use VISA: card number, expiration date and customer signature must be included.

Name _____

Address _____

City _____ State/Zip _____

VISA Card # _____ Exp.Date _____

Signature _____ 1146-18

The Artificial Intelligence Gang has a talent for getting into trouble... and a real genius for getting out of it!

Read all three books in

Bruce Coville's
A.I. Gang trilogy.

OPERATION SHERLOCK

The A.I. Gang is born when six brilliant kids are swept up in a hurricane of action as they try to prevent an evil spy from sabotaging their parents' top-secret computer project.

ROBOT TROUBLE

The A.I. Gang can handle space satellites and singing robots —no problem. But when they get mixed up with real death threats and murderous masterminds, it spells trouble for the whole gang!

FOREVER BEGINS TOMORROW

The A.I. Gang faces the ultimate showdown with their most dangerous enemy ever: the mysterious Black Glove. Not only are the Gang's lives at stake— so is the future of the whole world!

Available from Minstrel ® Books
Published by Pocket Books